Date Due

AUG 30 '98			
AUG 02 '99			
JUN 06			
JUN 27	WITHDRAWN		
AUG 1 9	Damaged, Obsolete, or Surplus		
OCT 0 5	Jackson County Library Services		
DEC 1 0			
JUN 1 1 '02			

Father   Mother   Dan

Dinah

Nicky

Davy

Donny

Daisy

Copyright © 1998 by Nord-Süd Verlag AG, Gossau Zürich, Switzerland
First published in Switzerland under the title *Pauli Wo ist Nickel?*
English translation copyright © 1998 by North-South Books Inc.

First published in the United States, Great Britain, Canada, Australia,
and New Zealand in 1998 by North-South Books,
an imprint of Nord-Süd Verlag AG, Gossau Zürich, Switzerland.

Library of Congress Cataloging-in-Publication Data is available.
A CIP catalogue record for this book is available from The British Library.

ISBN 1-55858-899-X (trade binding)
TB 10 9 8 7 6 5 4 3 2 1
ISBN 1-55858-900-7 (library binding)
LB 10 9 8 7 6 5 4 3 2 1
Printed in Belgium

For more information about our books, and the authors and artists
who create them, visit our web site: http://www.northsouth.com

Don't miss the other books about Davy and his family:
WHAT HAVE YOU DONE, DAVY?
WHERE HAVE YOU GONE, DAVY?
WILL YOU MIND THE BABY, DAVY?

What's the Matter, Davy?

Brigitte Weninger
Illustrated by Eve Tharlet

Translated by Rosemary Lanning

A MICHAEL NEUGEBAUER BOOK
NORTH-SOUTH BOOKS / NEW YORK / LONDON

Davy loved his toy rabbit, Nicky. Nicky had long floppy ears, dangly legs, and a little round body, and Davy never went anywhere without him. They slept together at night and they played together all day. They paddled in the stream, played in their secret den in the forest, and floated bark boats across the pond. When it was time to go home, Davy always tucked Nicky into the hood of his cloak and hopped back to the burrow.

One day Davy came home, took off his cloak, and reached into the hood. But Nicky was not there! Davy gasped in horror.

"I must have dropped Nicky," he told his mother. "I'll have to go back and look for him."

"All right," said his mother, "but don't be long. It's nearly supper time. Take Donny with you. He'll help you find Nicky."

Davy and Donny
looked in the rushes
at the side of the stream.
They looked in the forest,
and all along the paths,
but there was no
sign of Nicky.

"Oh, no, where can he be?" said Davy.
"Come on, Davy," said Donny.
"It's getting dark. Let's go home.
We'll find Nicky in the morning."

Mother had made a big pot of vegetable stew.
It was delicious, and everyone had second helpings,
except Davy. He wasn't hungry.
"What's the matter, Davy?" asked Mother.
"I thought you liked vegetable stew!"
"How can I eat," said Davy, "when Nicky
is out there, alone in the dark?"

Davy couldn't get to sleep. He tossed and turned in his bed.
"What's the matter, Davy?" whispered his big brother Dan.
"I can't stop thinking about Nicky."
"Don't worry," said Dan. "I'll help you find him tomorrow."
Then Daisy lent Davy her doll. "So you won't have to sleep
alone tonight," she said.
"Thank you," said Davy. He snuggled down under the blanket
and hugged Daisy's doll, but he still could not sleep.

In the middle of the night, Davy crept into his parents' room.
"Mama," he sobbed, "what if I never find Nicky?"
Mother Rabbit held him tight until he stopped crying.
Then she whispered, "Tomorrow we will all help
you search. I'm sure we will find him."

In the morning the whole family went out to look for Nicky.
They searched high and low, but found no sign of him at all.
"Poor Davy," thought Mother.
   She hopped back to the burrow and took out her sewing basket.

When Davy came home, looking tired and sad, his mother
called him. "I have something for you," she said. "It has long
floppy ears, dangly legs, and a little round body."
"It's Nicky!" cried Davy. "You found him!"
"No, Davy, I'm sorry. It's not Nicky. I made you a *new* toy rabbit."
She gave it to Davy.
"There. Do you like it?"
"Yes, Mama. Thank you, Mama," said Davy quietly,
and he gave his mother a kiss.

Davy took his new toy rabbit to bed with him.
It was the same size as Nicky.
It was as soft and cuddly as Nicky.
It looked as clean and bright as Nicky
used to look, when he was new.
But it was not Nicky.
"Maybe I just need to get used to you,"
Davy said. He laid the new toy on his pillow,
sighed, and went to sleep.

Days passed, and Davy finally gave up looking for Nicky. He picked up his new toy and went out to play in his den in the forest.
The sun was shining, flowers were blooming, and high above Davy's head a bird was singing. It sang so beautifully that Davy looked up, and he saw . . . something blue!

It was Nicky, caught in the fork of a branch.

"Nicky!" shouted Davy. " What are you doing up there?"

Davy stretched and gently lifted Nicky down.

Then he hugged him very tight.

"Nicky. My Nicky," he whispered.

Then he ran all the way home.

That night Davy went to talk to his mother.
"I've thought of a name for my new toy rabbit," he said.
"It's Dicky!"
"How nice," said his mother. "Nicky and Dicky."
Davy looked thoughtfully at the two toy rabbits.
"You know what, Mama?" he said. "I'm lucky to have
two toys, but I can't help loving one of them best."
Mama smiled.

Davy went over to the crib where
his little sister Dinah lay, waving her arms in the air.
"Look, Dinah, this is Dicky," he said. "You can have him."

"I hope you'll love him as much as I love Nicky." Then Davy kissed
Dinah good night, and hopped off to his own bed, where he
cuddled Nicky in his arms and fell fast asleep.